THIS BOOK BELONGS TO

....

Written by Tim Bugbird.
Illustrated by Nadine Wickenden.
Designed by Annie Simpson.

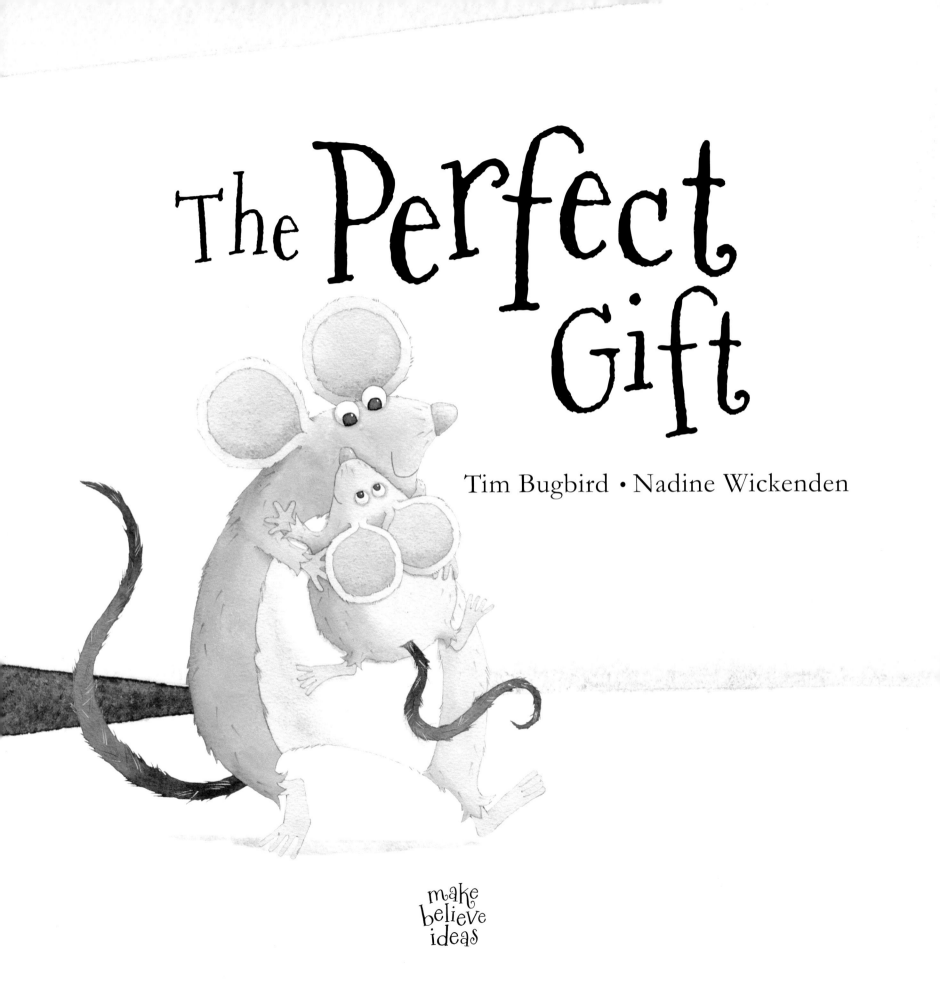

The Perfect Gift

Tim Bugbird • Nadine Wickenden

make
believe
ideas

Three days before Christmas,
Little Squeak was playing
in the forest when he
saw a beautiful acorn.
"This will be the perfect gift
for Big," he thought.

Little Squeak carefully wrapped the acorn in a golden leaf and hid it in the hollow of an old tree trunk.

On Christmas Eve, Little Squeak collected the acorn.
But just moments from home, it slipped from his paws,
rolled into the stream, and was washed away.

"I'm sorry," he said to Big.
"I lost your gift and have nothing
to give you for Christmas."

"But you have already given me so much!" replied Big.
"Dry your tears, and I'll explain . . ."

The **gift** you give has no **shape** or **size**.
It's the **love** that I see
when I look in
your **eyes**.

It's the way that you laugh

when I tickle your toes . . .

and the **smile**
on my face
when you **wrinkle**
your **nose.**

It's not tied with **ribbons**,

and it doesn't

look **grand.**

It's the **trust** that you give

when you take my **hand**.

Your gift isn't fancy,

but inside, it glows bright.

It's the warmth

that I feel when we

cuddle up tight.

It's beautiful music – my own special sound.

It's the song in my heart

when you are around.

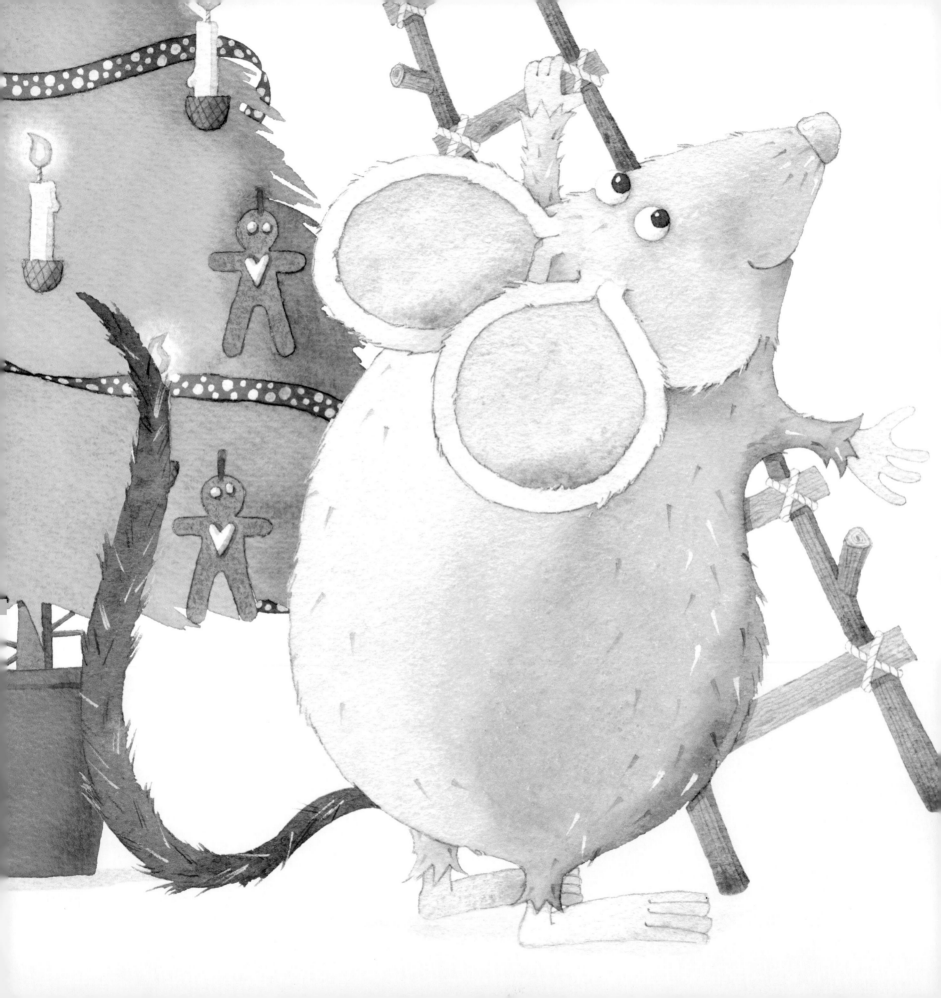

When there's only one left, but you say,

"This is yours,"

you give me much more

than is held in your paws.

And as time passes by, it's a gift to know

I'll receive such joy

just watching you grow.

So we'll hang up our stockings,

but remember what's true . . .

I have **all**
that I need;
the **perfect gift**
is **you!**

In the distance, a clock struck twelve; it was Christmas Day.

Little Squeak and Big looked up at the stars.
"Thank you," said Little Squeak.

"Thank YOU," said Big.

THE END